W9-CNA-242

SAINTS AMONG THE ANIMALS

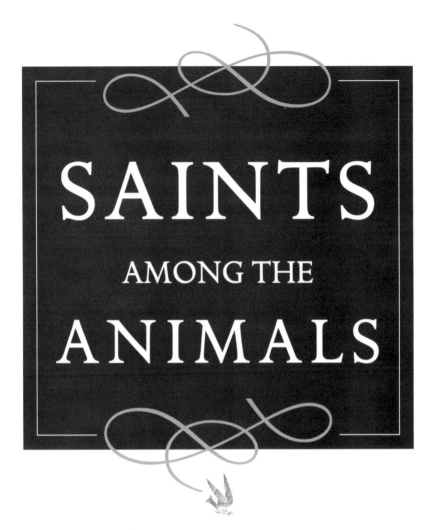

SAINTS

AMONG THE

ANIMALS

CYNTHIA ZARIN

WITH ILLUSTRATIONS BY

LEONID GORE

A RICHARD JACKSON BOOK
ATHENEUM BOOKS FOR YOUNG READERS
NEW YORK + LONDON + TORONTO + SYDNEY

For Beatrice

Atheneum Books for Young Readers • An imprint of Simon & Schuster
Children's Publishing Division • 1230 Avenue of the Americas, New York,
New York 10020 • Text copyright © 2006 by Cynthia Zarin • Illustrations
copyright © 2006 by Leonid Gore • All rights reserved, including the right of
reproduction in whole or in part in any form. • Book design by Kristin Smith •
The text for this book is set in Goudy Old Style. • The illustrations for this
book are rendered in charcoal. • Manufactured in China • First Edition •
10 9 8 7 6 5 4 3 2 1 • Library of Congress Cataloging-in-Publication Data •
Zarin, Cynthia. • Saints among the animals / Cynthia Zarin; illustrated
by Leonid Gore.—1st ed. • p. cm. • "A Richard Jackson book." •
ISBN-13: 978-0-689-85031-8 • ISBN-10: 0-689-85031-X • [1. Christian
saints—Biography—Juvenile literature. 2. Animals, Legends and stories of—
Juvenile literature.] I. Gore, Leonid. II. Title. • BX4655.3.Z37 2005 •
270'.092'2—dc22 • 2004007259

CONTENTS

AUTHOR'S NOTE

Several years ago I came across an old small blue clothbound book, called *Saints Among the Animals*. The text was by Margaret Ward Cole, the pictures— primitive, charming woodcuts—were by her husband, Alphaeus Cole. It had been printed in 1905 by The Green Sheaf, London. I later learned Alphaeus was the son of Timothy Cole, the English engraver.

The stories were direct, moving, and simply told. They took hold of me. I began to read more about the lives of the saints, but as I did, I found myself returning to the stories of saints and animals, until I realized I had begun to think of how to tell the old stories myself. The result is this book.

I am indebted to Margaret Ward Cole for the title and for her book. Other sources include, particularly, *Beasts and Saints*, by Helen Waddell; *The Oxford Dictionary of Saints*, third edition, edited by David Hugh Farmer; *Lives of British Saints*, by Sabine Baring-Gould and John Fisher; and *Lives of Irish Saints*, by J. Hanlon. Any mistakes or conflations are my own.

✳

THE STORY OF SAINT COLMAN

A long time ago in a lonely part of Ireland where the green cliffs meet the white waves, there lived a monk called Brother Colman. Colman liked to talk and laugh, and to make life pleasant for himself and his fellow priests by telling a good story or a joke as he worked in the garden among the radishes and turnips, or as he scrubbed the long table where the monks took their meals. Often the faces at Colman's table were the happiest under the monastery's low-pitched roof, and many times voices raised in song reached up to the rafters and startled the brown wren who made her home there.

As in other years, summer gave way to autumn with its scudding clouds. Winter came, and the white waves froze, rearing up like strange beasts, each one wilder than its neighbors. Days grew short and the nights dark, for the sun had taken shelter from the bleak wind on the other side of the earth—yet its far-off rays always seemed to shine brightly where Colman was.

But one day during the cold months when he was pulling the last of the winter vegetables, a hand descended over the monk's brow and covered his eyes so that everything before him was cast in shadow. "What has come over me?" asked Colman, much afraid. The hand was featherlight and did not hurt him, so rather than strain against the dark, Colman shut his eyes.

At first all was black. But as he stood in the garden he saw a growing brightness, like the moon rising. In it he saw the faces of his mother and sisters, whose house he'd left as a young man, once he knew that he was meant to live his life in the service of God. The faces of his childhood friends shone in the sky above them like stars. Then Colman saw the figures of his fellow monks, now his everyday companions—one brother whitewashing the fence by the priory, another sweeping the floor under the long table—and then he saw all of them at prayer, heads bent before dawn, and then again when the sun set over the wild sea.

How he loved them all! And so Colman saw, with the feathery hand still light on his brow, that in his habit of constant laughter he had neglected, a little, his duty to God. And he saw too, as the deft hand over his eyes lifted and the garden glinted again in the late-afternoon sun, that he must leave even this remote windy spot where he lived with his brothers, and retreat to a farther place.

A green hill with a crown of hawthorn trees lay half a mile inland, away from the monastery, and it was there that Colman built his hut of stones. "Don't go," cried his brother monks, for they knew they would miss him sorely. But

when they saw he was in earnest they said good-bye, and watched as, carrying only his small load of books, he made his way to his hut on the hill.

Soon there was a path through the high grass in the meadow, for Colman came once a day to fetch his bread, which the monks left for him in a cloth by the door, and each day the brown wren who lived in the rafters shed a tear, for she knew how lonely he was without companions.

One morning when Colman was lying in bed before the dawn it happened that a cock appeared at the window and with his hearty voice bade the monk good morning. "Good morning to you!" said Colman. And he pulled on his slippers in a hurry, for if not for the rooster's greeting he would have been late to say his morning prayers. At breakfast Colman saved a few crumbs of bread and left them on his windowsill, in hope that the rooster would come again to share his solitude.

Was there a man happier than Brother Colman when he opened his eyes the next day to
the crowing of the cock? From that time on, the
rooster made himself at home at Colman's window, eating what bread the monk could spare
(Colman himself, as you might imagine, ate less
so as to have more to share with his friend), and
he never failed to wake the monk in time for his
dawn prayers.

A little while after, a small gray mouse came
too, to make her home with Colman. Her games
pleased him greatly, for she liked to run and hide
behind a chair and peep out at him suddenly,
and Colman, who was quick with his hands,
made her a ladder out of thread. To his delight
she learned to climb it, and to jump from one
chair to another. In the evening as dusk fell the
cock and the mouse would chatter together, and
in turn nibble at the pieces of bread Colman
had saved for them.

Colman took great joy in his new friends,

and he gave thanks to God, who had sent them to ease his loneliness.

Besides the company of his fellow creatures, Colman loved to read, and it was because of this pursuit that a fourth came to join the trio. One day a storm suddenly blew up over the sea and drenched the meadow, and Colman rose in haste from his book, without marking his place, to close the wooden shutter he had made for his window. When he returned, he found, to his surprise, that a bluebottle fly was waiting patiently on the page, at the very word where he had stopped reading. Colman was astonished, and shook his head, thinking it must be happenstance. But soon he began to trust in the fly, and he never thereafter marked his place in a book, confident that it would be held for him until his tasks allowed him to take up his reading again. And some-times too, while the monk was reading, the fly would settle on the page at a place of particular interest, so that Colman would take note and read it again!

So passed the days of the monk now called Saint Colman, because of his obedience to God and the delight he took in his fellow creatures, especially his staunch companions, the cock, the mouse, and the fly, whom he loved dearly.

SAINT WERBURGE AND THE GEESE

n the north of England, near Chester, the soil is rocky, the sun barely shines, and the farmers who sow their seeds in that earth have a hard time of it. One spring, a long time ago, their job was made harder still, for a huge flock of geese landed on their fields and ate up everything the farmers planted.

The geese were so many that when they rose up to fly their wings blocked the sun and clouds. But rather than go after they had eaten their fill, the geese waited until the farmers tried to plant their wheat and barley and gobbled the seeds up again.

What a terrible state of affairs!

It so happened that many of the fields tilled

by the farmers were on land that belonged to the Northamptonshire convent. Not knowing where else to turn, the farmers decided among themselves to visit the abbess there, Mother Werburge, and ask for her help.

The next morning the men washed their hands and faces with special care and cleaned their boots, too, and set off for the convent. There they were welcomed very pleasantly and asked to wait in the Great Hall. Soon a vast iron-work door opened and Mother Werburge came forward. The abbess was tall and her face was gentle. Watching her approach, the farmers felt their hearts lift for the first time in many weeks.

"What can I do for you, good men?" asked Mother Werburge, smiling at each farmer in turn.

They began to answer all at once, interrupting and tripping one another up in order to tell their tale, looking for all the world like a gaggle of geese themselves.

After a few minutes Mother Werburge, who

had remained quiet while the farmers squawked and squabbled, raised her hand. The men fell silent. She turned and said to the least talkative farmer, "Go to the field and round up the geese. Tell them that I said they will come see me here."

The farmers began again to talk at once, protesting loudly that the geese would not come, but the farmer the abbess had addressed, whose name was Alaric, bowed deeply to her and went on his way.

It had rained that morning and the fields were wet. Where this time of year there should have been green stripes of sprouting wheat, all was muck and mud and the pronged footprints of geese. The geese themselves, grown as large as new lambs on their gorging, were clumped here and there, poking in the earth for any seeds they might have missed.

Alaric shook his head at the scene. Then, although he had little hope in his heart for it, he did as the abbess had asked and spoke to the geese, his voice never rising above his ordinary friendly tone. "You are wanted, all of you, by Mother Werburge in the courtyard of the convent. She bids you make haste."

A great noise rose up from the geese, along with much heaving of wings by those who were clearly vexed. But in a moment, to Alaric's astonishment, the birds began to move, not in a line, but in one mass of waddle and feathers, in the direction of the convent.

What a sight! Women making bread came out of their houses, their arms floured up to their elbows; children gaped and pointed; and one little boy followed after the flock, collecting enough feathers from the muddy lane to stuff a pillow.

The gates of the convent were open, and as the geese approached Alaric dropped behind, shepherding the fowl into the courtyard in twos and threes. Then, as Werburge had left word that he do, he shut the gate leaving the geese within, and went home to his family.

Night came on. The penned-up geese, left to themselves, muttered darkly to one another, and by morning—hungry, worried, and afraid— they called out with honks and cries to Mother Werburge that they were truly sorry for their terrible deeds and begged her to release them.

The abbess had listened all night for their cries, and when she heard the birds' pleas she came down to them and said, "You have been punished now by your misery and fear. You may go if you promise never to return to this place again and never again to steal seed or grain, nor trample the fruit of men's labor."

The geese thanked her, stretching open their beautiful wings, but when they made to go, a tremor went through the crowd, and they gathered around Mother Werburge with downcast expressions.

She bent from her height and knelt among the geese, to hear them better, and when she rose her face was stern.

"Who has done this?" she asked, and a servant of the convent came forward to admit that she had indeed made a goose stew the previous night for her supper. "And good it was, too, ma'am," she said, whereupon the abbess turned on her and upbraided her for harming a guest in her house.

"Bring me the bones from your feast!" she commanded her.

The servant departed and came back with a sack of bones. Werburge took the sack in her arms, and in a thrice there was a rustling of beating wings and the missing goose leapt out to join her friends.

Such a great chaos of applause and jubilation! Then Mother Werburge nodded, and the geese, in orderly procession, left through the convent gate, each bowing to her as they passed, and flew off, never to be seen in those parts again.

SAINT FRANCIS
AND THE WOLF OF GUBBIO

f you go now to the town of Gubbio in Italy, you will see the peaceful piazza before you, planted with flowers. There are a few cafés and a bakery, its window boxes overflowing with pink geraniums. In the morning the piazza fills with the population on its way to school or work, and at noon, with those hurrying home for lunch. By four o'clock the piazza buzzes with the sound of motorbikes and children playing ball around the fountain. In May comes the crossbow festival, which people travel from miles around to see.

It was not always so. There was a time long ago when the town was gripped by terror. When the butcher and the baker went to bed at night, they knew not which of their stock would be missing by morning. Chickens, pigs, and cattle shuddered in their barns, and mothers, waking at night trembling, checked their sleeping children twice or even three times before the cock crowed. By day people went about their business, whether drying fruit or scratching sums, but a cloud hovered over them even when the sun shone.

A wolf was the cause of all this trouble. Terrible creature, he lived in a cave above the town ramparts where brambles grew wild and the grass was sharp as thorns. It was a cold and lonely place, where stones and boulders lost their footing, and treacherous to walk near, lest a hail of rocks come falling down.

The wolf, loathsome in his habits, was bothered by none of this. Gray, foul-smelling, he slept by day in his littered den and lived only to creep out at night when, unmindful of all but his own appetite, he slunk through the streets and stairwells, lying in wait for goat and goose alike and the moment he might spring on them and sink his teeth.

Now it so happened that the monk later called Saint Francis, who traveled often in his region of soft hills near Assisi, came at this time of terror to preach the word of God and remind the townspeople of their duty to the poor and hungry, as he had done before.

By nature the people of Gubbio are genial and generous. But as Francis, on foot, approached the Porta degli Ortacci, the town's main gate, he met only gaunt faces drawn by a pen dipped in worry, who barely offered a greeting and whose eyes darted fearfully right and left.

"What is the trouble, my good Giacomo?" Francis asked a shepherd who was urging his sheep through the gate with a nervous nod. "Why do you look so grave?" And he gestured to the flute in the shepherd's belt, for he knew the man of old and how he loved to play.

"Oh, no," said the shepherd, following his

gaze, "I dare not make music now, for the wolf might hear and find me."

By then a small crowd had gathered around the monk and the shepherd, eager to hear what their beloved Francis might say. There was Antonio the farmer, with sheaves strapped to his back, and old Luisa, with her apron full of chestnuts. Caio the baker shifted from foot to foot under his load. And there were others not known to us by name. All stood silent, waiting for Francis to speak.

"Take me to him, this wolf," he said, his voice strong and clear. "I will speak to him where he lives."

There was much objection from the crowd, who cried out as one saying, "No, do not go there." Luisa, who had known Francis since he was a child, pleaded particularly. But once he set his mind to something, Francis could not be swayed, and the little group, which grew larger as the news of his intent spread like a flame in a haystack, was resigned and decided to follow him, for they knew not what else to do.

"Play your flute," said Francis to Giacomo the shepherd, "and show the wolf we fear him not."

And so the little procession made its way up the limpid hill, the fields alight with the yellow flowers the people there call *ginevre* and we call wild ginger. Autumn bees hummed in the gold air, and a herder in the valley could be seen tending his white oxen attentively, his hand on his staff.

Up, up, they climbed, yapping dogs running circles around them. Giacomo played his flute. Francis was quiet, and as they climbed the little parade quieted too, until even the dogs were silent. The air chilled and clouds gathered.

"There it is," said the shepherd in a hushed, frightened voice, stilling his tune. He pointed to a dark place in the hillside where the rocky ground was littered with trash and bones.

"Do not be afraid," said Francis. But as he moved toward the cave no one came with him.

"Oh, do not go!" cried Luisa, trying one last time to dissuade him.

Francis did not turn, but walked steadily forward, and when he came to the place where rubbish despoiled the earth, he picked his way neatly among it. He stood a moment. Then he began to speak, and although he was some way off from the huddle of townspeople, the wind that had picked up and was now flapping their garments carried his words back to them.

"Oh, Brother Wolf," he said, "come out! I am here to speak with you as a servant of God who rules the heavens and the earth."

The wind rushed up for a moment, churning the dry leaves about, and the little group of onlookers huddled closer together. Then it was quiet, as if the hills themselves were listening.

"I know you are hungry, Brother Wolf," said Francis in his low voice. "It has been a hungry season for you, for the sun shone hard and parched the fields. Now winter is coming and

your appetite is great. I know what that is. But the Lord tells us that when our appetites are quelled, we will receive what we need many times from Him. Come with me, and I promise you will be hungry nevermore." Francis paused in his speech and then said, almost beseechingly, his words like an echo of the flute's melody in the still air, "Come out, Brother Wolf, come out!"

Lo and behold, to the amazement of the people gathered, the wolf—dirty, covered with sores, his bones like knives under his fur—crept out of his lair. And if that weren't enough, he stood on his hind legs and embraced Francis, who did not shrink from him.

Then, as if to further confound all reason, the wolf lay down at the monk's feet, and Francis said to him, "Now you must repent, for you are a thief and a murderer, and have brought terror to the hearts of these good people who have done no harm to you."

To the crowd's astonishment, the wolf

bowed his head, and with the ragged procession trailing behind (for they were still a little afraid), he followed Francis down the hill through the gate of the town and told the people there of the pact he had made.

And from that day forward the wolf never hurt a flea, but was obedient to Francis's order, and, like any penitent friar, begged for food and was given it. So pleased were the people, who talked ceaselessly of what they had seen, that they grew to love the wolf, for he was a reminder in their midst of their beloved Francis, and when the wolf died he was mourned as one of them.

A STORY ABOUT SAINT MEDARD

he kind and absentminded monk Brother Medard lived more than one thousand years ago in a very beautiful part of France, where the pastures are bounded by swift streams, where in summer grapes hang like jewels from the vine, and the woods are busy with foxes and chipmunks, with birds and every sort of butterfly. Medard later became the bishop of a great cathedral, at Noyon, but this story is from the time before, and it tells why Medard is known in France as a saint for wet weather. There's even a rhyme about him that people still say near his birthday, which is in June:

> *S'il pleut le jour de Saint Medard,*
> *Il pleut quarante jours plus tard.*

This means that if it rains on his birthday, it will rain for forty days afterward.

Here is the story. More than anything else, Medard loved to take long walks in the country-side, and when he could, once he had finished his tasks, he would tramp off, often accompanied by a few friends, into the meadows beyond the town. One June day when it was especially fine—the sky was the color of a bluebird's wing and the climbing roses cast their tresses up into the trees—Medard went for a walk with some bread and cheese and two companions. They walked and walked, hardly taking note of the distance they traveled, for the conversation was interesting to them all. When they came to a hill, the top of which would offer them a view of the countryside they loved, they climbed happily up.

It was just then, in the pine forest near the top, that they felt the first few drops of rain, and when they arrived at a clearing and looked down across the plain, they saw that a violent storm was breaking close by and would soon be upon them. As people sometimes do, Medard's companions behaved as if fire, not water, were falling from the sky, and they turned right around and ran down the hill. But Medard stayed put. He looked across the valley, admiring with his whole heart the plumes of dark clouds and listening to the leaves tell him about the adventures of the approaching wind. Finally, his mind full of what he had heard and seen, Medard made his way without haste down the hill. And though rivulets of water ran down the path beside him and the leaves glistened, he forgot the storm entirely until he reached his own doorway and found his friends waiting for him, soaked to the skin.

But rather than greeting him, his wet companions pointed and stared with surprise. And what did they see? An eagle, his huge wings

outspread, had traveled with Medard all the way home, keeping him warm and dry!

Medard was much moved by the eagle's attention. While the rain kept up, the eagle would not leave his station above Medard's head, but soon the storm tapered off and stopped altogether. The monk put out his hand to thank the bird, and immediately the eagle folded his wings and came to perch on Medard's outstretched arm. Medard then gave him the bread and the cheese that had not been eaten on their walk and thanked the eagle for his protection.

And from that time forward, when Medard went for his walks in the countryside, he never brought along any clothes for wet weather because at the first sign of rain the eagle would appear to serve as his umbrella.

A FEW SHORT TALES
OF SAINT CANICE

ow, Brother Canice was born in County Derry in Ireland, the son of a bard who liked nothing more than a good song, and so for the rest of the monk's life he sought nothing more than silence. He early left the house of his noisy family and dedicated himself to the service of God, joining the monks first at Clonard and then at Iona.

But since he was bred to it, he was never able to forgo congenial company entirely. He was torn between the joy he found in his friends and his quest for solitude. After his visits hither and yon, he retreated, paddling his dory to one island or another in the Firth of Lorn, where but for the wild creatures who flocked to him, he was alone in the still and the quiet and could immerse himself in his translation of the Gospel.

Even then, though, he was pestered. Once on the island called Ich-Unish the mice nibbled so furiously at his shoes that he lost patience, took one off, and threw it at them. Of course, it landed in the water. He had to hop on one foot all the way down to the sea to retrieve it, and as he did he spoke severely to himself, saying it was a judgment upon him for treating the mice so harshly. When he returned with the dripping shoe, he apologized to the creatures very humbly, and such was their regard for the monk whom they loved that they vanished and were never seen to plague anyone on that damp knob of earth again.

Another time—it was a Sunday—on the island of En-Inish, Canice thought the chatter-ing birds might drive him mad. He bade them to be quiet in a gentle voice, rather than in the stern tones that first occurred to him. Replying, the birds who had been circling overhead, screeching and conniving and interrupting his morning prayers, all came down together to the ground by his feet, and bowing their beaks to their breasts, they listened to his offices, remaining quiet until the next day, when the Sabbath was over.

And here is one more story about Saint Canice. In the small wilderness of his island retreats he liked to read as he picked his way through the gorse and the bracken, holding the book before him. But sometimes the book he held was heavy, and he grew tired. At these times there was a stag who lived in the green wood who would come to him, as if he had been waiting and watching from his thicket of leaves, and loom up before Canice to offer his great antlers as a bookstand.

Once while Brother Canice stood reading God's word with the patient stag, a loud retort in the woods startled the animal, and he bounded

off into the forest with the book lodged in the crook of his latticed crown. But soon he returned, like a fugitive monk to his abbot, the book unharmed and the page unturned, and the monk went on happily reading.

A STORY ABOUT SAINT HILDA

The village of Whitby, in Yorkshire, sits on a hump that shoulders its way into the North Sea. A little river opens at Whitby, but as it peters out on the moors, not many boats make use of it. Sometimes the winds there are so fierce that chunks of the cliff, as if pulled by a giant claw, are hurled down to the beach. And even now, if you pause to turn over those pieces of rock, you will see that they are among the strangest on earth. For on the surface of these stones and inside them—whichever way they crack open, and you can do this with a hammer—are circles and whorls, as though a finger had drawn shapes there endlessly. Here is why.

High above the village, where the houses

huddle together before the wind, is Whitby Abbey. While some below might look up and shake their heads, the sisters who lived there, almost fifteen hundred years ago, would abide no other place. They loved the long view of the sea from their windows and the hazel carpet of moors that stretched to the west. The sound of the sea accompanied them as they went about their work, and in the morning and evening they listened for the answering hum of the tide as they sang. In the village the baker and the black-smith heard the plainsong carried down to them on the quick air along with the smell of gorse.

But none loved the moors and the sea more than Mother Hilda, the abbess, who had been bred in that country. Often, as a girl, she had run off to explore the moors and the cliffs, learning to know the pipers, the shrews, and the beetles, and while the sight of a hawk with a bloodied mouse in its claws did not trouble her, the sight of a trap surely did. If she came across a trap set in the hawthorn she undid the latch and set any poor, caught, terrified creature free. Her parents warned that if she persisted in her walks she must take a spade against snakes, but she would not. On the contrary, there was a serpent she counted as a particular friend, who lived near where the river waxed from trickle to stream and to whom she brought the small creatures she found that were beyond saving.

The village of Whitby was especially dear to Hilda, because for many years she had been gone from it, in the service of God to the abbey at Hartlepool. When she was called home with her band of sisters, her joy in returning was felt by all of them, so that work out of doors— tending to their small flock of sheep, drying fish in the wind, sowing the vegetables that thrived in the salt air, and supervising the bees—was the most coveted.

But too soon after Hilda's return all happy activity came to an end. One by one—and why should this be?—the sisters shied from the out-doors. The first was Sister Helena, who came one morning to Mother Hilda, looking pale, to ask if she might stay within the abbey. Hilda wondered at this, for the morning was crisp, and it was often Helena who came in late from her walk down to the sea, with her skin fresh and her eyes shining.

Next was Sister Catherine, the abbey gar-dener, who simply bolted from the kitchen garden, back into the scullery, and ran upstairs without pausing to even wipe her hands.

Then there was Sister Agnes, who one morning was not seen at all. A report was brought to Mother Hilda that Agnes, known to be healthy and stout of heart, had turned her eyes to the wall and would not leave her bed.

"What am I to do?" Hilda asked herself as one after another the sisters refused to leave the abbey walls. And though she asked each one in turn what was the matter—for now Sister

Margaret, Sister Frances, and Sister Bridget had joined the ranks of those who not only barricaded themselves indoors, but who refused to come downstairs—there came no answer. The sisters shuddered and turned white, but they said nothing.

"What can this be?" asked Hilda as one week stretched into two, then three.

It was April, and the sun was warm on the earth. Yet the kitchen garden remained cracked and hardened by winter, and instead of a house of the spirit, the abbey seemed full of ghosts, for the pale nuns, trembling, paced the long floorboards of their sleeping chamber as if in a trance.

"We will starve!" exclaimed Hilda, not without cause, one night at supper in the refectory as she and Sister Magdalen, each sitting at an end of the table with all the places in between now empty, made a meal of the last of October's windfall apples. "Perhaps the Lord has in mind that I should till the garden myself," she continued, "and although I am happy to comply, it will take more hands than mine and yours together to keep us fed."

Hilda shook her head and looked down the scrubbed table at her companion, expecting an answering nod, but instead, to her great surprise, she saw that Magdalen had risen to her feet and was standing in horror, pointing a shaking finger.

"What is it?" demanded Hilda, rising to her full height and looking at where Magdalen stood like a quaking leaf.

"*See! See!*" said Sister Magdalen.

And when Hilda looked at where the sister was pointing, she saw that from under the serving plate, a snake had lifted its head and was gazing at her with his obsidian eyes as if he would speak.

"Is this the trouble, then?" asked Hilda gently.

"Yes," said Magdalen, who, when she saw Hilda standing steady, calmed herself, for she trusted the abbess above all else. "I had prom-ised not to say. But the serpents are everywhere.

Under the rocks in the garden and on the sea-wall, in the crevices of the abbey stones, in the wheelbarrow curled up tight, in the straw in the cowshed. But they do not come where you walk, and the sisters were afraid you would think they saw what was not there. And they are so sorely terrified that they are not sure by now if the snakes are really there or not, or which is worse, for if the serpents truly are abroad, the sisters are ashamed before you to be afraid."

Hilda was silent. Then she said, quietly, "They should not be afraid of me." Fiercely, she turned to the snake. "Be gone," she said. "Do not come again inside the abbey. And let it be known that I will speak to all of you."

In answer, the snake slipped off the table and disappeared through a chink in the wall to the garden.

Then Hilda addressed Magdalen. "Tell the sisters they, too, are to make themselves ready to hear me."

A sunny space by the west wall of the abbey faced away from the sea. Beyond it stretched the moors, wave after wave of green traced with rivulets of water. Within minutes, Magdalen came again to Hilda, her habit billowing in the wind, followed by a line of downcast sisters, who trailed behind like knots on a bedraggled kite string.

When they were assembled, Hilda stood by them, but with her back turned, and raised her arms toward the moors in a gesture of entreaty.

"Come out," she said, "and show yourselves!"

And from all over, the land began to rustle and move, as if a wind had started to blow not over but under the earth. From every place there—from the gorse, the trees, around the fence posts, by the gates—the snakes rose up as one.

Behind Hilda came a muffled cry as Sister Agnes fainted.

Hilda did not turn. She folded her arms and addressed the crowd, her voice strong and clear. "I am flattered," she said, "that the brethren of my old friend the serpent should seek me out, now that I have returned to the place of my birth. He was a confidant and gave me much good and steady counsel. But I cannot have you abide with me here. Our cow will not give milk, and our land is lying fallow."

There was much swaying and consulting among the snakes, and as they spoke to one another, their tongues made a rasping sound. Then one of them came forward, and behind Mother Hilda, the sisters shrank back.

Hilda bent her head to listen. "No," she said, shaking her head. "I beg you now to leave this place." And she pointed her finger to the farthest edge of the horizon, beyond what could be seen.

The rustle began anew. On the periphery a few creatures took themselves off to the cliffs.

"I am sorry," said Hilda. She raised her hands a final time, but the benediction she gave astounded all who were present. For when she dropped her hands, every one of the snakes who would not leave had turned to stone.

And that is why, if you walk on the shingle beach below the cliffs at Whitby, you will find the strange shapes of snakes in the old stones the wind tosses there.

THE STORY OF SAINT KENETH

 very long time ago in Wales there lived a prince and his wife, both of whom longed for a child. They waited and waited, until each feared, in secret, they would turn gray without one. So great was their joy when, one summer, twins were born to them.

At first both boys seemed quick and vigorous, but it wasn't more than a week before the old nurse, who had cared for their father before them, saw that the child they had named Keneth was odd and misshapen. One of his legs was shorter than the other, and his poor back was bowed. She went to his mother and said, "He will not walk, ma'am."

There was much crying and lamenting and wondering what to do, but before anything could happen, the nurse, who practiced the old ways, wrapped the baby in swaddling clothes, put him in a little boat made of osiers, and set it in a stream that rushed merrily to the nearby sea. Then she told his mother the baby was dead.

The child, of course, knew none of this. It was a warm day and the sun dappled the water. Snug and warm, the baby had no reason to be afraid. He mewed a little to the breeze, but after a while, as no one answered, he began to cry.

Now, if you were to look at the sward where the deep green land comes down to the water, you would think it empty, but it is not. Many creatures live there. Chief among them are the gulls. They fly everywhere and see everything, making a racket, so at first when they heard the child crying, they thought the sound was of their own making. (And how many mothers by the sea have been woken by the cry of a gull and gone to their own child's bed, thinking he was calling to her?) But when the gulls saw the little boat drifting toward the open water, they took pity, plucked the baby up gently, and took him to an empty nest, high up on the cliff.

It was a large nest, sheltered from the wind. To make it soft for the child, the birds gathered grass from the headland, and a few added what feathers they could spare from their own downy breasts. One stood guard over the child at all times, and each took his turn at it.

All this was very well, but what was the boy to eat? Gull babies eat fish snatched from the icy water and winkles broken up on the rocks, but that wouldn't do for a human child.

There was a doe who came to the stream every day to drink, and as she had lost her fawn, she agreed to give milk. But then what to put it in? Nearby, the gulls, who have an eye for anything that glitters, spied a bell by the green bank, with its rope neatly attached (in some stories, they say it was left by an angel), which made a perfect receptacle.

And so the baby lived happily in his nest. When the wind blew, the birds protected him with their outspread wings, and he grew strong, fed by the milk they brought him every day to drink.

Things continued this way for some time, until one bright morning when a shepherd whose sheep had strayed heard, over their fussing and bleating, what sounded to him like a baby's cry. Being a father himself, he rushed to find the source of the sound, thinking a village child might have toddled off and fallen into a crevasse. Great was his astonishment when he saw Keneth, basking in the dawn, fingering the sunbeams as if he were playing a pipe.

But the moment the gulls saw the poor man, whose name was Gildes, they swooped at him, jabbing him with their beaks lest he come near their charge. He persisted stoutly, for he knew it was his duty. He scooped the child up in his arms and made off with him as fast as he could, sure he was saving the boy from being eaten alive.

What else could he do? Gulls screaming at him with every step, he brought the baby to his hut and gave him to his wife. Now, she had raised three of her own, and it took only one look for her to know that the child was lame. Nevertheless, she was kindhearted, and she resolved to keep him.

All that day and the next the gulls screeched overhead, crying, "*Give him back! Give him back!*" until the shepherd and his wife wondered, hands over their ears, if the child was bewitched. On the third morning the shepherd's wife was hanging out the linen to dry. The baby lay on a blanket beside her. But the moment she turned her back to pin up a cloth, two gulls swooped down and, each grasping a corner of the blanket in their strong beaks, carried the baby back to their aerie. And though the shepherd and his wife grieved for him, they agreed between themselves that his snatching was the will of God.

So Keneth grew in the nest, tended by gulls who loved him. They could not teach him to fly, but they began to carry him down the cliff to the beach, and by the time he reached his full height, he could walk quite ably with a stick and tend to all his needs himself.

In a place cut out of the rock, he built a hut from wood washed up from the sea. There, on his rising up and lying down, he gave thanks to God. His was the only voice he knew, and as he listened well, he heard many things and learned how to live in his solitude.

But nothing under the stars is a secret. One by one, fishermen from the nearby village began to catch glimpses of him, returning with reports of his coat made of feathers and of the pot shaped like a bell from which he ate his meals. In time the people began to wonder about him.

They tried to think out who he might be (for the shepherd had shared his story among them). Wherever he walked, they said, the gulls and the sandpipers accompanied him, following behind, for all the world like pages behind a prince.

Soon the stories spread far and wide, until even Father David, the abbot of Pembrokeshire, learned of the hermit who lived by the shore and kept company with birds. He came to visit Keneth himself on his travels and, seeing he was crippled, bade him to stand before him. Keneth did, leaning on his gnarled stick, and David (whom we know as Saint David, the patron saint of all Wales) took the stick from him and said, "Behold, he walks."

And to the amazement of those who were with David—the monks from his monastery at Henllan—Keneth stood straight as a divining rod on dry ground. But rather than rejoicing in his good fortune, he hung his head before David and asked that his infirmity be restored to him,

for it was the source, he said, of his blessing. Without it, he would not have come to live as he did with the creatures of the sea and the sky, and because of it he could be as one with those most beloved by God.

David listened in silence; his eyes clouded over, and he did as he was asked. For the rest of his days Keneth limped along the stony edge of the beach, his presence easing the hearts of all who came to find him. When they came home, they bore their own burdens more lightly. After a time they said he was a saint among them, and that is how we know of him.

SAINT BRENDAN AND THE WHALE

he green waters of the Irish Sea are rough during the months of October and November, but that was no matter to Saint Brendan. One year, a very long time ago, he promised to preach with his friend Brother Malo in Brittany at Christmastide. So off he went with his band of sailors in their scow. Before they were out more than a day, the gales poured icy water over the prow with such force, it flew off the stern and wet the poor brothers on deck to the skin.

But Brendan was not deterred. After seven days and nights of harsh weather the brothers, stout sailors though they were, came to him and said, "Father, if we cannot put in to shore, we would rather a watery grave." And they pressed him to let them stop for a day and a night from their labors, for the coast was not too far.

Brendan was a big man, and jovial, even when cold and soaking wet. But though he tried to jolly them along, those hands that were on deck stared at him stonily. Hour passed into hour, but the sky did not lighten. In the hold a few sailors not bound to the Lord hammered away at a raft of their own devising, for they said they would not stay past gray dawn on that ship.

On deck in the gale Brendan paced, taking his turn at the watch, once calling into the dark, "If Thou does not see fit to lend me the sun, send me the moon, his sister, that I might find my way by night!"

No answer came, and it seemed they were done for. The black wind blew without ceasing, and the monstrous waves seemed likely to devour them altogether. But in the small hours, like a mule that has trod all day with head down, the scow suddenly stopped. *What might this be?*

thought Brendan, shuddering. *Let it not be the flint edge of a rock to break my poor ship in two.*

But as he lamented, his wonder grew, for the wind too had stopped, and a bright moon came out from behind the clouds like a lost sheep.

The silence woke the sleeping sailors one by one, and they staggered on deck, rubbing their eyes and looking about with amazement. Where for days they had ridden a sea that tossed up one nightmare wave after another, as tall as a church and warning of everlasting damnation so that each man shook in his sopping boots, now the sea was the color of lapis lazuli and dawn had rent the dark with gold. The boat had come aground on an island so small that from the deck they could see all the way around it. The still sea lapped quietly at its edges, and in the shallows was a school of tiny fish.

"Behold!" said Brendan. "Look what the good Lord has wrought." And he smiled a little to himself but said nothing more.

"It is a sign sent to us, Father," said Brother Malachi.

"A blessing on our journey," said another, who dropped to his knees on the glistening old deck, and all their number followed suit, a few speaking into their hands words of praise and prayer.

Could those words be the cause of what happened next? For when the men rose up and looked about, marveling at their good fortune—some making haste to pull off their sodden clothing and leave it to dry on the rigging, so that the boat turned suddenly gay, festooned with all manner of jerseys, stockings, and trousers—out of the dawn came a thousand small birds. They made no sound but the soft beating of their white wings.

The birds perched on the mast and the bow and the boom of the ship, and even on the shoulders of the brothers who stood bemused, for a feeling of peace had come upon the crew.

Some birds gathered along the shore of the little island, which was curiously without vegetation but for the sea bracken that clung to it, and were quiet, until together they began to sing a song that made the men think of stories they had heard long ago, of sirens who pulled sailors to the deep, and they were afraid.

"Witchcraft," came one voice, seconded by another.

Then, as if in reply, one bird, the largest among them, who had left the others and perched in the crow's nest, swooped down and gazed directly into Brendan's eyes, opening and shutting its beautiful wings, which made a sound like a bell.

"Who are you?" asked Brendan, much amazed.

"We are from the fall of the ancient enemy," said the bird, "a time when there was much destruction over the earth. We did no wrong then, but we did not aid the fight. Now we are lost souls, who wander always through the grace of He who did not annihilate us, but we cannot serve on Earth as we wish to do. On the Sabbath we assume this form and sing to those who can go forth and do His work. You may say to your brothers that your destination is not far, and at the end of your long journey you will be welcomed there."

With that the great bird paused and joined the others in song. They had lowered their voices while he was speaking, but now the singing rang out until the dark came, deep and blue, swallowing up all but the glow of the ship's lanterns. Then, with a lifting of wings, they disappeared into the night sky, replaced there by an equal number of stars.

The warmth of the day lingered, but soon the sailors, even in their dry clothes, shivered and made to build a fire on the small island where they were mercifully aground. As that odd place yielded no timber, the half-made raft from belowdecks was broken up and pressed into service.

Lo and behold! No sooner had they struck the first spark than the island twitched! And as the blaze began to burn the island bucked and heaved, like a thing alive!

In an instant those brothers who had gathered by the flame were on board, trembling. "What manner of island is this, Father?" they demanded of Brendan.

By this time the boat holding them all was afloat, for as the island shuddered, the sea rushed to cover it, and Brother Aidan, who was closest to Brendan and some say his confidant, was hoisting the sails.

"Do you not know what kind of place this was?" asked Brendan. The men shook their heads. "It is a great fish, such as swallowed Jonah. He likes sinners and thus was sent to rescue us."

And the brothers gazed in wonder, for the

island—such as it was—was swimming far out to sea, the fire on its back burning brightly, until some miles out it dove down to the bottom of the ocean, taking the blaze with it like the sun setting at evening time.

SAINT KEVIN AND THE BLACKBIRD

he place on Earth most dear to the monk we now know as Saint Kevin is called Glendalough, after the two blue lakes that lie one above the other on the slope of the green hill like a pair of raindrops on a leaf. Kevin was born and raised near there, in County Wicklow in Ireland, and from the time he was small, he liked best to sit patiently by the lower lake waiting for the small fish that came up to the surface to greet him and to watch the dragonflies skimming the ripples with their deft feet. His dear friend was a blackbird, who ate her meals from his hand.

Kevin's father was a man of business, and he had thought to rear up his sons to his way of life. But when day after day he saw Kevin by the lake rather than bustling about with his brothers, he gave care of the boy to the monks at the Wicklow abbey and asked them to teach him to serve God. Fond as Kevin was of his fellows—especially shy Brother Herriot, who worked in the scullery, and Brother Patrick, who taught him his letters—he bided his time, and whenever he could, he slipped away to his glade and Glendalough and his companions there.

Kevin was indeed lucky in his masters, for while the abbot knew of the boy's excursions, he never put a stop to them. There are many ways, he knew, to show devotion in the world God has made. When one October afternoon Kevin, now a young man, stood before him with a hazelnut leaf in his hair and a tear in his cassock where a briar had torn it, the abbot wasn't surprised to hear him ask if he might go and live in solitude at Glendalough.

How happy was Kevin when the abbot granted his wish, and with what joy did he pack his few things! The next morning it took no longer than a fraction of the sun's upward arc for him to bound through the meadow to his new home, and but an afternoon's work to build a hut from the fallen branches of a nearby stand of alder trees.

It was a snug house. But it was made stronger still by the secret work of the black-birds, who are the best nest builders, and who in the night brought all manner of straw and wattles and wove them tight into the roof as a present for their friend who had finally come to live among them. When Kevin awoke and saw what they had wrought his eyes filled with tears. He thanked the birds as best he could, leaving out crumbs from his loaf and saving out a certain portion always for his old friend, whose wings were turning gray now, though she still had strength to hop up and eat from the young monk's hand.

But no amount of straw and wattles could

keep the glow of Kevin's presence from illuminating the place. When dusk fell, the stars came out to see his rival light, and as time passed they began to speak so often to one another of his goodness that word of it spread far and wide. There were rumors, too: A cow lost from her flock had found her way to Kevin's hut and returned to the barn and given milk tenfold. When Kevin despaired of how to feed a baby given to him for safekeeping (this is another story, and a true one), a doe appeared out of the brush and nursed the child until he was weaned.

Poor man, he loved his solitude, but it wasn't long before it was broken by the faithful who began to seek him out, camping under the alders, washing their clothes in the lakes, and frying fish for supper on the trampled grass! One day even the abbot himself appeared, mopping his brow from his hike up the hill through the meadow, for he had heard of the crowd and wanted to see for himself.

But instead of banishing the followers and restoring Kevin's peace, the abbot took the crowd as a sign of God's intention that Kevin should live once more among his fellows.

Though heavy in his heart, Kevin obeyed. He came down with his adopted son, Brian, the one nursed by the deer, to help with the building of a new monastery. Out of love, Kevin called the place Glendalough, and the monks who gathered there around him became renowned for their gentle ways and their devoted service to God.

But every morning when he woke for morning prayer and each night when he lay down his head, Kevin thought of how he longed to return to the lake and his hut by the alders. Days turned into months and months to years. The seasons wizened Kevin but left his longing untouched, and it finally happened that one day his work at the monastery was done. Bent now and leaning on a stick (for Kevin lived, we are told, to be more than one hundred years old), he retraced his steps slowly up the green slope, his footprints marking the start of the final words of his story.

When at last he arrived, he found, to his surprise, that his house was intact. The birds, who loved him and never gave up hope of his return, had been vigilant in their mending and kept his hut for him so that he could live there until his soul might ascend to God. The alders, too, were still standing, except for one felled by a storm so recent that the break in the wood was still white and fresh. A blackbird, who so reminded him of his old friend that she might have been her great-granddaughter, pecked anxiously around his gnarled feet, full of solicitude for his journey.

Kevin was so happy to be once more in the place that he loved, he dropped his stick and held out his arms as if to embrace the day with praise and thanksgiving. And as he did so, just imagine, the little blackbird at his feet flew up, nestled in his outstretched hand, and laid an egg! For it was the tree that had held her nest—and her great-grandmother's before her—that now lay on the ground. And so loving and steadfast was Kevin that he made his hand into a nest for her. There he stood, his palm open, his knobby back unbent, his heart sturdy, through wind and pelting rain, until the egg hatched and the little bird flew free.

SAINT JEROME AND THE LION

t was twilight in the Syrian desert of Chalcis, and the pitched sky, pierced with stars, was the dark blue color of water. Under this tent of shadows Father Jerome sat reading aloud to a group of monks who huddled by the fire. Books of learning and scripture lined the walls of his stone hut; piles of books rose precariously from the scrubbed floor, and seldom did a day pass without a crash from within Jerome's lair, followed by a cry of outrage. The towers often toppled, and Jerome was known for his temper.

While he read, the sky turned from blue to black. It was a still night, and all was quiet but for Jerome's voice and the whisper of turning pages, until, first far away and then growing near, a rustling sound came from the underbrush. At first the monks took no notice. There are many small creatures in the desert that are nocturnal by nature. But soon the sound distinguished itself from the others— a thumping, dragging noise—and one by one, they began to feel afraid.

"What can it be, Father?" asked Brother Joachim, seated close to Jerome, who had paused in his reading to listen. As one, they all peered into the darkness, until, in some tall grasses a little way off, they could see—oh, fright and horror!—the great head of a lion— oh, peril!—emerging.

The heart of each man jumped into his throat, and his feet leapt off the ground to follow. Jerome rose and said evenly to the trembling monks, "Wait and be still."

And because the men loved Jerome, and even feared him a little, they listened, although they longed to flee.

There was a clearing before the patch of

grasses, and when the lion came into it with the new moonlight behind him, his face was stern, but his great head was bowed, his mane full of brambles, and his gait unsteady.

"Look and see," said Jerome, the only one among the monks who had not covered his face in fear. "The beast has hurt himself."

And when they took their hands from their eyes, the other men saw that he was right: a thorn was grievously piercing the lion's paw, and he was limping.

Who can know why the wild creature came as a supplicant there, and to Jerome? For all who saw the spectacle say that as the lion approached him, there passed between the two—the fearsome beast and the cantankerous monk—a long look of understanding such that those who looked on ceased to be amazed, even when the lion knelt in front of Jerome and held out his paw.

"Fetch me a bowl of water and some

bandages," said Jerome to Brother Damasus. As soon as it was said, it was done, and then it was Jerome's turn to kneel beside the beast. With a tenderness never seen before in him, he pulled out the thorn, which he put by, and wrapped the lion's paw in bandages.

"Now go yonder," he said to another monk, "and fetch some straw for our guest. He is weary and needs to lie down."

So they all retired—Jerome and the beast, too. On the next day and after that the lion did not leave the side of his benefactor and made clear he intended to stay with him always. But Jerome spoke to their guest, saying, "If you remain here, you must work as we do, for to be idle is a disgrace unto the Lord. There is a donkey who fetches firewood from the forest. You will accompany her on her rounds and make sure no harm comes to her."

The lion happily complied, and it was a sight to see the meek donkey and the great beast head off together at daybreak and return when the sun began to set, chatting to each other all the while.

But then a terrible thing happened. One midsummer afternoon when the air was heavy with flies, the donkey and lion gathered their quota of firewood more quickly than usual, and so, taking advantage of their unexpected leisure, the donkey, her head circled with a crown of butterflies, set off to graze what she could from the nettles. And the lion, after making sure no predators lurked nearby, settled down under a dry copse to sleep.

Unlucky day! For it was just then that some merchants on their way to market were passing, and spying the nibbling donkey seemingly untended, they crept up on her from behind and made off with her.

Well, you can imagine how the lion felt when he woke up from his slumber! His fear like a stone thrown in a lake, he loped in ever-widening circles searching for his charge, calling her name in his low, gravelly voice. But he could find no trace of her. Even their load of wood had vanished, for the merchants had taken it for their own fires.

It was night when the lion, heartsore, gave up his search—and the gloom did not lessen as he returned home, for the monks were going about their evening chores in the thickening dark without fires to warm them or light their way.

Rather than going into the monastery as had become his custom—for he was too sad and guilty for that—the lion hid himself instead in the tall grasses from which he had first appeared. There he crouched peering through the sharp blades to the place where Jerome was reading aloud by candlelight.

"Where can they be?" the monk asked, pausing in his text and looking about. At this the lion came out and stood alone before him.

Immediately a loud clamor rose up from those assembled.

"He has eaten her!" cried Brother Antinicus,

who loved the donkey dearly and whose job it was to care for the animals about the place.

"I told you so!" said Brother Tobias, who had always been afraid.

But as before, Jerome raised his hand and they fell silent. "The beast is our friend," he said, "and he has been steadfast. It is not for us to judge before the Lord. Tomorrow you will make haste to discover what misfortune may have come upon us."

And he bade his fellows good night, motioning to the lion that he should sleep in his customary place.

The next morning the sun rose yellow as an oxeye. The day was bright and clear. Like notes scribbled down the margins of a story, the monks traversed the borders of the country looking for traces of their beloved donkey, often in their zeal bumping into one another and circling over the same swath. As night fell, though, they could only shake their heads, for they had found nothing, yet they fell on their supper with vigor and afterward appealed to Jerome to decide what to do.

"The poor beast is more chastened than any of you," he said, and his dark look dared them to contradict him. "See how he languishes and will not touch his food? But as before, he will not be idle. As it was on his watch that our helpmate disappeared, he shall assume her chores and go forth each day himself to fetch us kindling."

The lion bowed obediently, and so it was that the regal beast each day lowered his head for the harness and performed the menial task.

Winter came, and the ground grew stony underfoot. The wood cracked easily into kindling, but there was less of it to be found and the monks needed more and more to keep warm in the icy weather. The lion's labor lengthened. He lingered later, and it was at one such late hour that he heard bells tinkling.

Startled, for it was seldom that anyone came to that place, the lion climbed a nearby promontory to get a better look. And what should he see coming toward him but an untidy procession of camels and wagons, with a few men in dusky robes walking alongside and others riding—and at the head of it a donkey, pulling her load!

Well, it took only a moment for the beast to see that this was his lost friend, as everything about her was dear to him, down to her blue halter, frayed now, which the lazy thieves had not bothered to change. In a flash he was upon them, exultant, propelled by a mix of rage and rapture. The animals and men who saw that they could not escape cried out terrified, repenting as they looked death in the face.

The lion did no harm, but rather ran circles around the caravan, by turn roaring at those who tried to flee and telling the donkey how glad he was to see her, until, as by some plan, she turned in her tracks and began to pull her load in the direction of the monastery, and the lion brought up the rear, herding those who sought to hide in the darkness.

Such rejoicing was there when Brother Antinicus found his donkey returned to him! But looks grew grave as one by one the monks came out to see, until finally Jerome himself appeared and sternly surveyed the thieves, who looked down and pawed their feet on the ground like the donkey they had shamefully stolen.

Jerome was so angry that he bit his tongue to keep from speaking, and thus it was one of the thieves who spoke first. "Please, Father," he began. "We are sorry we have strayed and want to make amends. Each time we pass, we will give you four liters of the oil that we sell at the market."

"No!" Father Jerome thundered. "You shall not be easily forgiven! Be gone with you, and let the Lord be your judge!"

And seeing his wrathful face, the ragtag band, leaving the donkey behind, made their way into the darkness.

A silence fell over the monks. The moon illuminated their faces as if it were daylight.

Brother Damasus, fingering his cassock in a worried way, lifted his eyes and gazed at his angry old friend.

"It is not our way, Jerome," he said.

Then Jerome did not speak, but gave a curt nod to Antinicus, who ran off into the dark. It was only a few moments before he returned with the merchants, for the way was difficult and they had not gone very far.

"We accept your offer," said Jerome. "Now go with God."

So the procession trudged off, until the sound of camel hooves was tamped down by distance. From that time forward, the monks never lacked oil, even in lean times, for the thieves kept their word. Their fires burned brightly, fed every day by the little donkey and her protector, who kept one eye open even as he slept. At night the lion, whose pallet was now at the foot of Jerome's bed, often listened as the monk read aloud, and some say he grew as wise as his master.

BIOGRAPHIES

Saint Colman was born in Ireland at Kiltartan, joined the monastic order in Aramore, and is venerated as the bishop of the monastery in Kilmacduagh, which he founded on land given by King Guaire of Connacht. He died in A.D. 662.

Saint Werburge is reputed to be the daughter of Wulfhere, king of Mercia. A number of English nunneries were either founded or administered by her. She was buried in Hanbury, in Staffordshire, circa 700. Twelve ancient churches are dedicated to Werburge.

Saint Francis of Assisi was born in 1181 in Italy, to a wealthy merchant. As a young man, he renounced his inheritance, including even the clothes he had on, and turned to a life of charity and poverty. The Franciscan order of friars bears his name. His Canticle of the Sun was written in 1224, and he died in Assisi in 1226.

Saint Medard, born in Picardy to a noble family, joined the priesthood in 502. The bishop of Vermandois, he died in 560. On his feast day a village girl is crowned with roses in church and given a prize, usually money. In addition to his affinity with weather, he is the patron saint of those who suffer from toothache.

Saint Canice, an Irish abbot, was born in County Derry circa 525. He founded monasteries in the north and south of Ireland, but spent years of his life as a hermit on lonely islands copying books, including a manuscript of the Four Gospels. He died circa 600.

Saint Hilda, the abbess of Whitby, was born in 614 and entered the monastic life when she turned thirty-three. The abbey, which she founded in 657, was renowned as a center of learning, and it was she who encouraged the cowherd-poet Caedmon to write his verses. She died in 680.

Saint Keneth, also known as the Welsh saint Kyned, was born in the sixth century. There are two stories about him, which may have been conflated. In one story he is the son of Gildas, the abbot who founded the monastery at Morbihan, in Brittany; in the other he is the crippled son of a king, whose cradle of osiers brought him to the island of Henisweryn, in Wales. His feast day is celebrated in Wales, Brittany, and England.

Saint Brendan, the abbot of Clonfert, was born circa 486. Also known as "The Navigator," he was based in western Ireland, where he also founded monasteries in County Clare, County Galway, and County Kerry. *Navigation of St. Brendan*, written in the ninth or tenth century by an Irish monk, recounts his fantastic ocean voyages. Saint Brendan died circa 575.

Saint Kevin was born in the sixth century. As a young man, he lived as a hermit at Glendalough, where today there is a cave called "St. Kevin's Bed." He founded the monastery there and reputedly lived to be 120 years old. He died circa 618.

Saint Jerome was born in Strido, Dalmatia, circa 341. He was extraordinarily learned, reading scripture in the original Hebrew and translating it into Latin. He also translated from the Greek. His travels included time in Constantinople and Rome, as well as his desert sojourn. He died in Bethlehem in 420.